# Primetime Parable Ministries

PRESENTS

# the Mayberry Bible Study

## volume 2

### study guide

WRITER: *Stephen Skelton*

CREATIVE: *Jim Howell, Judy Northcutt Gaertner*

# The Mayberry BIBLE STUDY, *volume 2*
# PUBLISHED BY *Primetime Parable Ministries, LLC*

Scripture quotations taken from the HOLY BIBLE, NEW INTERNATIONAL VERSION. Copyright © 1973, 1978, 1984 by International Bible Society. Used by permission of Zondervan Publishing House.

Written materials are creation of author and not endorsed by actors, producers, creators or copyright holders of television show.

Printed in the United States of America

ISBN 0-9717316-3-2

To order or receive more information: *1-877-GOD-IN TV (1-877-463-4688)*

# INTRODUCTION

## *Biblical Basis*

To illustrate a principle, Jesus often used a parable—an earthly story with a heavenly meaning. Parables allow listeners to recognize real-life events as relevant examples of spiritual truth. In this way, these short stories link what we already know to what we should believe. Those that resist only hear a trivial story, while those that look past the surface find meaning.

## *Scriptural Precedents*

In the parables, Christians have a precedent for utilizing stories for testimony. Interestingly, whether Good Samaritan (Lk 10:30-37), Lost Son (Lk 15:11-32) or Unforgiving Servant (Mt 18:23-35), parable characters did not proclaim the Good News. Indeed, our soap operas today feature similar dramatic narratives. Yet Christ used these secular stories to convey Gospel Truth.

In another direct example, Paul used references from the popular culture to communicate a spiritual message when he cited certain poets (Ac 17:28) and named the unknown god (Ac 17:22-24). In fact, when Paul said, "'Bad company corrupts good character'" (1 Co 15:33), he was quoting a line of dialogue from a theater play (Greek comedy *Thais* written by Menader).

## *Modern Parables*

Because the Bible is the most influential book in the world, modern writers borrow from it more often than we might think, whether they realize it or not. One fundamental way to use popular entertainment to engage a Christian worldview is to evaluate the story events from a Scriptural perspective. Even a casual conversation about a TV show can afford an opportunity to witness.

To identify God's purposes, first we should examine the overall program in terms of Biblical themes. Next, we should focus that lens on story lines, characters and names. Lastly, we need to use that information as a testimonial tool: mention what a character said about the Lord; uncover the Biblical meaning behind the names; then share how you were saved.

## *The Mayberry Bible Study*

Already, many of you have used this study to successfully reach adults, young people, non-church members—even to refresh the world-weary souls of longtime believers. For those new to the study, ask yourself… Do you want to engage and energize your class… Do you want to bring Jesus to searchers "where they are"… Do you want to model the powerful parable approach of Christ… Then you can use *The Mayberry Bible Study*.

Blessings,

Stephen Skelton
Primetime Parable Ministries

## ABOUT THE AUTHOR

**Stephen Skelton**, founder of Primetime Parable Ministries,
serves as host for *The Mayberry Bible Study*. Previously, he has served
as a writer-producer with Dick Clark Productions and later as head writer for
the television program *America's Dumbest Criminals*. As a Christian in the
entertainment industry, Stephen seeks to identify God's purposes in popular entertainment.
Stephen lives in Nashville, Tennessee with his wife and daughter.

## ABOUT PRIMETIME PARABLE MINISTRIES

At Primetime Parable Ministries, we believe many stories that transcend social,
racial and cultural barriers today do so because they contain spiritual truth
for which all people have a God-given hunger. Accordingly, the ministry promotes
a grassroots approach to using popular entertainment to engage a Christian worldview.
To that end, we hope these Bible studies not only provide a time of good fellowship,
but also continue to equip the church with ways to reach the world beyond.

# TABLE OF CONTENTS

## THE STORY

This episode, *"The Big House,"* preens with pride—right before it takes a fall—when Barney builds up the small-town courthouse into a big-time jailhouse to impress some captured cons! But when the crooks execute a few not-so-great escapes, it's up to Andy Taylor to humbly bring them back. In this case, the punishment is its own reward when the offender Fife commits the crime of pride!

## THE MORAL OF THE STORY

*This lesson, "The Pride of Fife," highlights the Biblical principle of Pride. The notes examine the way in which pride blinds us from seeing stumbling blocks. The lesson also illustrates why God deserves the glory for our accomplishments. The point of this study is that you should take pride in mainly one thing: Jesus thought you important enough to die for.*

# *the* Mayberry *Bible Study*

## *volume 2 • lesson 1*

EPISODE TITLE: **"The Big House"**

LESSON TITLE: **"The Pride of Fife"**

BIBLICAL THEME: **Pride**

# LESSON ONE
# "The Pride of Fife"

## Unit Overview

## Parable

*The Moral of Mayberry...*

PROVERBS 16:18

*Pride goes before destruction, a haughty spirit before a fall.* (NIV)

## Reflection

*At the Fishing Hole...*

GALATIANS 6:4

*Each one should test his own actions. Then he can take pride in himself, without comparing himself to somebody else* (NIV)

## Action

*Get Out Your Bullet...*

GALATIANS 6:14

*May I never boast except in the cross of our Lord Jesus Christ, through which the world has been crucified to me, and I to the world.* (NIV)

# Pride

> PROVERBS 16:18
>
> ***Pride goes before destruction, a haughty spirit before a fall.*** *(NIV)*

For most of us, pride is a blindfold that keeps us from seeing stumbling blocks. With pride as our guide, we claim all the credit, disown any weaknesses and thus become ripe for a fall. After an accomplishment, it's normal to feel elated, but God deserves the glory. When the Holy Spirit fills us, we see the world's rewards as a cheap substitute for God's glory. You should take pride in mainly one thing: Jesus thought you important enough to die for.

## Parable

### *The Moral of Mayberry...*

This episode, pride ruled the roost, and Barney strutted like a rooster. Meanwhile, the hen house was full of foxes. Barney proudly talked the talk, as Andy humbly walked the walk. As did the crooks, who strolled out of their cells three times! For Barney, life at "the Rock" was a pride-filled fiasco—not that he learned his lesson. Briefly, describe how each person dealt with pride.

**Andy:** _____

**Barney:** _____

**Gomer:** _____

**Prisoners:** _____

**Lawmen:** _____

What is your most recent accomplishment?

How did it glorify God?

_____

_____

_____

_____

> James 4:6
> But he gives us more grace. That is why Scripture says: "God opposes the proud but gives grace to the humble."

*Pride is hard on a person. It distorts vision, confuses balance and trips us up. **While proud people put themselves above others—which only makes for a longer fall—humble folks receive grace (Jas 4:6).** Compare how Andy and Barney dealt with the crooks—and how the crooks dealt with them.*

What did Barney see in the situation with the crooks?

What opportunity did Andy see?

_____

_____

_____

_____

What made Barney easy to manipulate?

How could he guard against this weakness?

_____

_____

_____

_____

*Pride tells us we can do anything we want—
and that we're too good to do things we don't.
Yet, no matter what reason we give, the Lord judges
us by our deeds (1 Sa 2:3). By comparison, the humble
often do as asked simply to serve.  Consider Barney
and Gomer and the Christmas lights.*

Between Barney and Gomer, how did each deal with the
Christmas lights?  For each, why?

_____

_____

_____

_____

**1 Samuel 2:3**
"Do not keep talking
so proudly or let
your mouth speak
such arrogance,
for the LORD is
a God who knows,
and by him deeds
are weighed."

**The lesson of pride is taught by
disgrace (Pr 11:2).** *For the proud, humil-
iation is a stern but ever-ready taskmaster.
You can avoid this correction if you turn
from self-centered desires.  Release from
self-satisfaction comes when you put self
after God and others.  Humility brings wisdom.*

**Proverbs 11:2**
When pride comes, then
comes disgrace, but with
humility comes wisdom.

Why did Andy congratulate Barney at the end?
Did he do harm or good?

_____

_____

_____

# Reflection

## *At the Fishing Hole…*

GALATIANS 6:4

***Each one should test his own actions. Then he can take pride in himself, without comparing himself to somebody else*** *(NIV)*

1 Corinthians 4:7
For who makes you different from anyone else? What do you have that you did not receive? And if you did receive it, why do you boast as though you did not?

Proverbs 29:23
A man's pride brings him low, but a man of lowly spirit gains honor.

*Pride makes us slaves to comparison. It forces us to size up others—the less fortunate, the better for pride.* ***However, whether wealth, prestige or power, you don't have anything that wasn't given to you by God (1 Co 4:7).*** *Next time you want to compare, compare yourself to Jesus Christ.* ***His humility will inspire you to reject pride so that you can receive honor (Pr 29:23).*** *And each time you fall short of his glory, his love will comfort and encourage you still.*

Like Barney, have you had something to prove to someone? Give an example.

_____

_____

_____

Like Gomer, have you taken pride in how well you serve? Give an example.

_____

_____

_____

_____

*The two officers got blindsided by pride in the form of Deputy Fife. Barney was too focused on himself to pay attention to them. Pride in you is dangerous because of the damage you can do to others. **Instead, you should fear the Lord— then you will hate all evil behavior (Pr 8:13).***

Like the officers, have you been hurt by another's prideful actions? Give an example.

_____

_____

_____

Proverbs 8:13
To fear the LORD is to hate evil; I hate pride and arrogance, evil behavior and perverse speech.

*Andy worked hard—to give credit to others. Despite saving the day himself—twice in the morning, once again in the afternoon—he knew he couldn't do his job alone. **Likewise, you need God to enable you (2 Co 3:5).** After all, you cannot accomplish his calling by yourself.*

Like Andy, have you humbly deferred credit for your hard work? Give an example.

_____

_____

_____

2 Corinthians 3:5
Not that we are competent in ourselves to claim anything for ourselves, but our competence comes from God.

# Action

### Get Out Your Bullet...

GALATIANS 6:14

***May I never boast except in the cross of our Lord Jesus Christ, through which the world has been crucified to me, and I to the world.*** *(NIV)*

*Take pride in Christ. Pride in the entice-ments of the world will ruin you. Jesus saves you when you die to them and live in him.* **Both the high and the low should be glad that status doesn't matter to the Lord—wealth, prestige and power are not only hard to obtain but easily lost (Jas 1:9-10).** *God favors our eternal souls over our earthly status.* **On the day that the Lord alone will be exalted, the arrogant will be humbled and the prideful brought low (Isa 2:11).**

James 1:9-10
The brother in humble circumstances ought to take pride in his high position. 10) But the one who is rich should take pride in his low position, because he will pass away like a wild flower.

Isaiah 2:11
The eyes of the arrogant man will be humbled and the pride of men brought low; the LORD alone will be exalted in that day.

What will you mainly take pride in?

_____

_____

_____

_____

9

Who will you give credit for your accomplishments?

_____

_____

_____

_____

When you reject earthly pride, what will you receive from God?

_____

_____

_____

_____

What do you feel most proud of doing?
Is it for the glory of the Lord?

_____

_____

_____

_____

## THE STORY

This episode, *"The Loaded Goat,"* can be counted on to show what happens when people pass the buck—or buck the goat! When a billy-goat named Jimmy wanders through a town under construction, everyone is too busy until it's almost too late. It goes to show that you can't keep a good goat down—especially when he's just dined on dynamite and he's ready to ram! It's an explosive lesson in accountability!

## THE MORAL OF THE STORY

*This lesson, "Account Me Out," highlights the Biblical principle of Accountability. The notes focus on how being accountable means being responsible for doing God's will. The study also addresses how our disobedience can hurt others. The goal of this lesson is that we should bring honor to Jesus with how we live each day—wherever we go, whatever we do and whatever we say.*

# the Mayberry Bible Study

## volume 2 • lesson 2

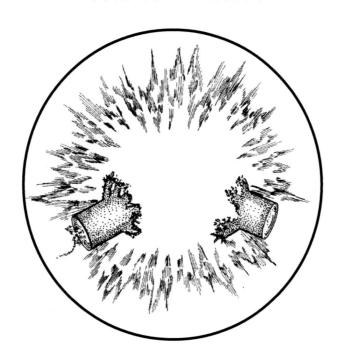

EPISODE TITLE: **"The Loaded Goat"**

LESSON TITLE: **"Account Me Out"**

BIBLICAL THEME: **Accountability**

## LESSON TWO
# "Account Me Out"

<u>Unit Overview</u>

## Parable

*The Moral of Mayberry…*

> ROMANS 14:12
> *So then, each of us will give an account of himself to God.* (NIV)

## Reflection

*At the Fishing Hole…*

> HEBREWS 4:13
> *Nothing in all creation is hidden from God's sight.*
> *Everything is uncovered and laid bare before*
> *the eyes of him to whom we must give account.* (NIV)

## Action

*Get Out Your Bullet…*

> COLOSSIANS 3:17
> *And whatever you do, whether in word or deed,*
> *do it all in the name of the Lord Jesus,*
> *giving thanks to God the Father through him.* (NIV)

# Accountability

ROMANS 14:12

*So then, each of us will give an account of himself to God.* (NIV)

Sometimes, buck-passing seems like the new national pastime. Today, most folks avoid accountability. But the Lord directs his people toward it. For a Christian, being accountable means being responsible for doing God's will. Because each person is accountable to God—not to men who can be deceived—we must take it upon ourselves to assume responsibility for our actions. Jesus did not avoid his responsibility and was held accountable at a most severe price.

## Parable

### *The Moral of Mayberry...*

Here, no one stood accountable for his actions, so almost everyone paid the price in the end. Hudge tied Jimmy up. Barney pushed Jimmy out. And Otis made him mad enough to ram—the straw that broke the goat's back. Not to mention, the Mayor denied the real reason he brought in dynamite! Briefly, describe how each person dealt with—or didn't deal with—accountability.

**Andy:** _____

**Barney:** _____

**Hudge:** _____

**Otis:** _____

**Mayor :** _____

What did you do last time a mistake was made?

How do you respond to blame?

_____

_____

_____

_____

***Accountability starts at the beginning—because our actions are judged in the end (Ob 1:15).*** *Make sure you feel fine with an open account of any action. Even actions done in secret are not hidden from God. Consider what the Mayor gave for an account and what he was accountable for.*

What did the Mayor say about the underpass? Would he have started if he had to tell the truth?

_____

_____

_____

_____

> Obadiah 1:15
> "The day of the LORD is near for all nations. As you have done, it will be done to you; your deeds will return upon your own head."

> 1 Corinthians 7:24
> Brothers, each man, as responsible to God, should remain in the situation God called him to.

*Being accountable means acting responsible.* ***God assigns you a place to do the work of his Word (1 Co 7:24).*** *If you don't assume responsibility first, you could suffer the consequences later. Think about how Hudge and Barney responded to Jimmy.*

What kind of owner was Hudge?
What could he have done differently with Jimmy?

How did Barney react to Jimmy at first?
As a result, what did he have to do a bit later?

*We're accountable for ourselves—whether we admit it or not. While blaming doesn't actually make others responsible, shirking our duty angers both them and God.* **To readily accept accountability, act in accordance with God's will and show others that you know him (1 Jn 2:3).**

How did Otis explain the fight with Jimmy?

How did Andy and Barney become accountable?

> 1 John 2:3
> We know that we have come to know him if we obey his commands.

**Romans 3:19-20**
Now we know that whatever the law says, it says to those who are under the law, so that every mouth may be silenced and the whole world held accountable to God. 20) Therefore no one will be declared righteous in his sight by observing the law; rather, through the law we become conscious of sin.

**1 John 2:4**
The man who says, "I know him," but does not do what he commands is a liar, and the truth is not in him.

**Proverbs 19:15-16**
Laziness brings on deep sleep, and the shiftless man goes hungry. 16) He who obeys instructions guards his life, but he who is contemptuous of his ways will die.

# Reflection

*At the Fishing Hole...*

HEBREWS 4:13
*Nothing in all creation is hidden from God's sight. Everything is uncovered and laid bare before the eyes of him to whom we must give account.* (NIV)

*The Lord knows everything about everyone everywhere. He knows all about us—and yet he still loves us.* **While you cannot earn salvation—that comes through the mercy of Jesus Christ—you can please God when you follow his will** *(Ro 3:19-20). It is your responsibility to obey his Word since your disobedience can hurt others. If you want more of his love, be accountable for more responsibilities.* **You can't say you know God if you don't do what he says (1 Jn 2:4).**

Like the Mayor, have you made your actions appear nobler than they are? Give an example.

_____

_____

_____

*Hudge and Barney dodged their duties—and the result literally came back to bite them!* **You should take every opportunity to be accountable because irresponsibility often carries a price—both here and in heaven (Pr 19:15-16).** *This is why God gives you guidance through his Word.*

Like Barney, have you avoided an opportunity to be accountable?
Give an example.

_____

_____

_____

_____


Like Hudge, have you paid a price for being irresponsible?
Give an example.

_____

_____

_____

_____


*Andy had to make up for a mistake he didn't make. Likewise, our selfish actions can cost those around us. When you obey God's Word, you live up to your personal responsibility.* **By contrast, your disobedience can hurt not only you but others as well (Jnh 1:8-9).** *For the sake of both, do what God wants.*

> Jonah 1:8-9
> So they asked him,
> "Tell us, who is
> responsible for making
> all this trouble for us?
> What do you do?
> Where do you come from?
> What is your country?
> From what people are you?"
> 9/ He answered,
> "I am a Hebrew and
> I worship the LORD,
> the God of heaven,
> who made the sea
> and the land."

Like Andy, have you suffered consequences
of another's irresponsibility? Give an example.

_____

_____

_____

_____

# Action

## Get Out Your Bullet…

> **COLOSSIANS 3:17**
> *And whatever you do, whether in word or deed, do it all in the name of the Lord Jesus, giving thanks to God the Father through him.* (NIV)

Proverbs 20:11
Even a child is known by his actions, by whether his conduct is pure and right.

*Do what you do for God. Your actions make you accountable.* **What you do reveals who you are, whether you are righteous or sinful (Pr 20:11).** *Sinful conduct can produce serious consequences—both for you and those around you.* **A good life demonstrates wisdom through deeds done in humility for others (Jas 3:13).** *As a Christian, consider what others think of Christ when they see you. Bring honor to Jesus with how you live each day— wherever you go, whatever you do and whatever you say.*

James 3:13
Who is wise and understanding among you? Let him show it by his good life, by deeds done in the humility that comes from wisdom.

Why will you be accountable?

_____

_____

_____

_____

_____

What will you be accountable for?

_____

_____

_____

_____

_____

What will happen when you follow God's will?

_____

_____

_____

_____

_____

_____

Are you comfortable being accountable?
Have you prayed about your actions?

_____

_____

_____

_____

## THE STORY

This episode, *"Mountain Wedding,"* marks the first
appearance of Ernest T. Bass—and the "T" stands for trouble!
Mr. Darling asks Andy and Barney for help when Ernest T.
tries to woo Charlene—who is already married to Dud!
While Andy tries to be the best man for the job, Barney ends up
in a wedding dress—and Ernest T. gives new meaning to
the name trouble-shooter!

## THE MORAL OF THE STORY

*This lesson, **"The 'T' Stands for Trouble,"** highlights the
Biblical principle of Trouble. The notes point out how trials
test faith—and when handled correctly—strengthen
perseverance. The study also explains that just as we are
not meant to rely solely on ourselves, we should offer help
to others in times of trouble. The core message here is that
if we only ask, God will help through faith, family and friends.*

# the *Mayberry* Bible Study

### *volume 2 • lesson 3*

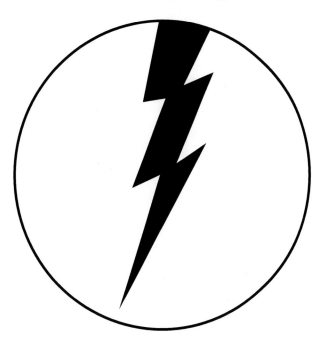

EPISODE TITLE: **"Mountain Wedding"**

LESSON TITLE: **"The 'T' Stands for Trouble"**

BIBLICAL THEME: **Trouble**

## LESSON THREE
# "The 'T' Stands for Trouble"

<u>Unit Overview</u>

## Parable

*The Moral of Mayberry...*

PSALM 46:1
*God is our refuge and strength, an ever-present help in trouble.* (NIV)

## Reflection

*At the Fishing Hole...*

JAMES 1:2-3
*Consider it pure joy, my brothers, whenever you face trials of many kinds, because you know that the testing of your faith develops perseverance.* (NIV)

## Action

*Get Out Your Bullet...*

JOHN 16:33
*"I have told you these things, so that in me you may have peace. In this world you will have trouble. But take heart! I have overcome the world."* (NIV)

# Trouble

**PSALM 46:1**

*God is our refuge and strength, an ever-present help in trouble.* *(NIV)*

When trouble comes, what we should fear is being too afraid to ask for help. Too often, because we feel overwhelmed or embarrassed in times of trouble, we think that no one would, could or even should help us. Trials test faith—and when handled correctly—strengthen perseverance. If we only make the effort to ask, God will always help us through our faith, family and friends. Remember this during the next time of trouble— whether you need help or are asked to help.

## Parable

### *The Moral of Mayberry...*

The answer to trouble is asking for help; even the Darlings knew that. But who knew such a small man could cause such big problems? While Ernest T. wanted to go out, Charlene wanted to stay home—married. So Mr. Darling asked the Sheriff to intervene—and Andy worked to satisfy both sides of the would-be wedding party. Briefly, compare how each person reacted to trouble.

**Andy:** _____

**Barney:** _____

**Mr. Darling:** _____

**Charlene:** _____

**Dud:** _____

**Ernest T:** _____

How do you respond when you are threatened?

Do you need the help of others?

_____

_____

_____

_____

*Got trouble? Call God—you've got a heavenly hotline through prayer.* **Whether troublemaker or peacekeeper, man can neither make nor encounter trouble too great for the Lord, the Maker of the heaven and the earth (Ps 121:1-2).** *Think how Mr. Darling and Ernest T. responded differently to trouble.*

How did Mr. Darling react to trouble?

Why did he feel comfortable asking Andy for help?

_____

_____

_____

_____

_____

Why did Ernest T. throw rocks, break windows and use guns? What did his actions say about his attitude?

_____

_____

_____

*Troublemakers react to trouble by making more trouble. They think they can overpower their problems. Peacekeepers search for agreement that satisfies both sides.* **Their comfort comes from God who comforts us so that we can comfort others (2 Co 1:3-4).** *Recall how Andy worked here.*

How did Andy offer to help in this situation? Which side did he try to satisfy?

_____

_____

_____

_____

*Trouble comes from selfish desire.* **Envy burdens both the envious and the envied. This is why God warns against coveting (Dt 5:21).** *To stop coveting, change your perspective and start being content. Rather than thinking of what you don't have, be thankful for all that God has given you.*

In the end, did Ernest T. change his attitude? What would he do if Dud mistreated Charlene?

_____

_____

_____

_____

2 Corinthians 1:3-4
Praise be to the God and Father of our Lord Jesus Christ, the Father of compassion and the God of all comfort, 4/ who comforts us in all our troubles, so that we can comfort those in any trouble with the comfort we ourselves have received from God.

Deuteronomy 5:21
"You shall not covet your neighbor's wife. You shall not set your desire on your neighbor's house or land, his manservant or maidservant, his ox or donkey, or anything that belongs to your neighbor."

# Reflection

### *At the Fishing Hole...*

JAMES 1:2-3

***Consider it pure joy, my brothers, whenever you face trials of many kinds, because you know that the testing of your faith develops perseverance.*** *(NIV)*

Ecclesiastes 4:9-10
Two are better than one, because they have a good return on their work: 10) If one falls down, his friend can help him up. But pity the man who falls and has no one to help him up!

1 Thessalonians 5:14
And we urge you, brothers, warn those who are idle, encourage the timid, help the weak, be patient with everyone.

*For Christians, trials come "whenever" not "if ever." God won't keep us from pain, but he will make us complete. He allows trouble so that we will turn to him and fellow believers.* ***Just as you are not meant to rely solely on yourself, you should offer help to others in times of trouble (Ecc 4:9-10).*** *To offer the most effective help, first understand the particular problem.* ***If you are sensitive to that certain situation, you can better suggest an appropriate solution (1 Th 5:14).***

Like Mr. Darling, have you asked for help with nothing to offer in return? Give an example.

_____

_____

_____

Like Andy, have you helped without expecting anything in return? Give an example.

_____

_____

_____

*When threatened, Dud was ready to go guerilla—warfare, that is.* **Christians who respond to threats with greater threats imply that the Lord won't take care of them. The cure to insecurity is confidence in God (Heb 13:6).** *He will help you solve your problems or give you strength to endure them.*

Like Dud, have you responded to trouble with threats of more trouble? Give an example.

_____

_____

_____

_____

Hebrews 13:6
So we say with confidence,
"The Lord is my helper;
I will not be afraid.
What can man do to me?"

*Ernest T. had a change of heart—and not just from Charlene Darling to Barney the Lady Sheriff.* **While a fool always wants a fight, a wiser man learns how to resolve conflict (Pr 20:3).** *Rather than seek security in your own strength, seek security in your unity with God and fellow believers.*

Like Ernest T., have you turned from troublemaker to peacekeeper? Give an example.

_____

_____

_____

_____

Proverbs 20:3
It is to a man's honor
to avoid strife, but every
fool is quick to quarrel.

## Action

### Get Out Your Bullet...

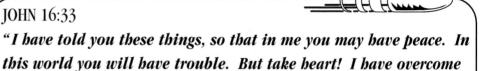

JOHN 16:33

*"I have told you these things, so that in me you may have peace. In this world you will have trouble. But take heart! I have overcome the world." (NIV)*

Psalm 7:16
The trouble he causes recoils on himself; his violence comes down on his own head.

Romans 8:35-37
Who shall separate us from the love of Christ? Shall trouble or hardship or persecution or famine or nakedness or danger or sword? 36/ As it is written: "For your sake we face death all day long; we are considered as sheep to be slaughtered." 37/ No, in all these things we are more than conquerors through him who loved us.

*Expect trouble. And expect to triumph. Tension comes from a fallen world at odds with the heavenly kingdom. Victory comes because Jesus does not leave us in our struggles.* **If you cause trouble, you will be destroyed by trouble (Ps 7:16). If you cling to Christ, nothing can separate you from his peace (Ro 8:35-37).** *During trials, look to the Lord for strength, help others find peace and remember that Jesus has already won the final battle.*

What will you do when you are in trouble?

_____

_____

_____

_____

_____

What will you do when others are in trouble?

How will you find the good in times of trouble?

What trouble are you worried about right now?
Have you asked for help?

## THE STORY

This episode, *"Andy Discovers America,"* teaches that sometimes teaching is best left to the teachers. When Andy tells Opie that history is hard, Opie hears that history is hardly worth hearing! Then Helen Crump sees the students stop learning, and she starts thinking about quitting school. As Andy attempts to correct his homework, everyone gets an education on the subject of teaching!

## THE MORAL OF THE STORY

*This lesson, "Teacher's Pest," highlights the Biblical principle of Teaching. The study concentrates on how God teaches us when we listen to him, learn his Word and obey his commands. The notes also point out how we teach others by our actions—both good and bad. In summary, this lesson shows Christ's plan for your life is that you communicate Christianity to commission others to teach more still.*

# the Mayberry Bible Study

## volume 2 • lesson 4

EPISODE TITLE: **"Andy Discovers America"**

LESSON TITLE: **"Teacher's Pest"**

BIBLICAL THEME: **Teaching**

## LESSON FOUR
# "Teacher's Pest"

### Unit Overview

## Parable

*The Moral of Mayberry...*

PSALM 143:10

*Teach me to do your will, for you are my God;*
*may your good Spirit lead me on level ground.* (NIV)

## Reflection

*At the Fishing Hole...*

PROVERBS 10:17

*He who heeds discipline shows the way to life,*
*but whoever ignores correction leads others astray.* (NIV)

## Action

*Get Out Your Bullet...*

2 TIMOTHY 2:24

*And the Lord's servant must not quarrel; instead, he must*
*be kind to everyone, able to teach, not resentful.* (NIV)

# Teaching

> PSALM 143:10
>
> *Teach me to do your will, for you are my God; may your good Spirit lead me on level ground.* (NIV)

Teachers and students agree, teaching is tough twice—it's tough to teach and it's tough to be taught. Yet, while we all need guidance in our lives, knowledge for its own sake is self-centered. We should ask to be taught to do God's will, not our own. God teaches us when we listen to him, learn his Word and obey his commands. Whether teacher or student, rather than ask God to answer every question, we should seek his overall direction for our lives.

## Parable

### *The Moral of Mayberry…*

Andy learned that teaching isn't for everyone after Opie got a lesson in the art of ignorance. When Opie said homework is hard, Andy agreed history isn't easy, and Helen Crump all but broke out the dunce hats for the Taylor boys. Meanwhile, Barney showed that a mind can be a terrible thing—if you don't use it. Briefly, describe how each person dealt with teaching.

**Andy:** _____

**Barney:** _____

**Opie:** _____

**Helen:** _____

**Students:** _____

Who have you taught—and what have you taught them?

Why do you want to learn?

_____

_____

_____

_____

> **James 3:2**
> We all stumble in many ways. If anyone is never at fault in what he says, he is a perfect man, able to keep his whole body in check.

*Good intentions don't excuse bad teaching. Good teaching centers on what you say—as well as what you don't say.* **Teachers must not only say the right thing at the right time, but also stifle any urge to say things they shouldn't (Jas 3:2).** *Consider what Andy did and why Helen got so mad.*

Did Andy give Opie bad advice? What could he have said better?

_____

_____

_____

_____

_____

Was Helen right to get so mad at Andy?

What should Andy have said back to her?

_____

_____

_____

_____

_____

*Learning requires real effort; listening just requires ears. **If we pay attention, God will teach us through the Bible, the Holy Spirit and our relationship with Jesus Christ (Jn 6:45-46).** Being open to God's teaching may mean actively seeking his direction. Recall how Opie listened and what he learned.*

Was Opie a good student or a poor student?
How much of the responsibility was his?

_____

_____

_____

_____

*It's never too late to teach or learn—no matter our age or station in life. **In fact, only by continually reading God's Word, do we begin to see God's will (Ps 25:5).** We never outgrow our need for the Lord's guidance. A man's years mean nothing next to God's timeless message.*

How much should Barney have known already?
Was it all right for him to learn too?

_____

_____

_____

_____

John 6:45-46
"It is written in the Prophets: 'They will all be taught by God.' Everyone who listens to the Father and learns from him comes to me. 46) No one has seen the Father except the one who is from God; only he has seen the Father."

Psalm 25:5
guide me in your truth and teach me, for you are God my Savior, and my hope is in you all day long.

# Reflection

*At the Fishing Hole...*

> **PROVERBS 10:17**
>
> **He who heeds discipline shows the way to life, but whoever ignores correction leads others astray.** *(NIV)*

**Luke 17:1-2**
Jesus said to his disciples: "Things that cause people to sin are bound to come, but woe to that person through whom they come. 2) It would be better for him to be thrown into the sea with a millstone tied around his neck than for him to cause one of these little ones to sin."

*We teach others by our actions—both good and bad.* **When you act badly, you teach others to sin. It would be better for you to drown in the sea (Lk 17:1-2).** *When you act rightly, you teach others to teach well.* **This is Christ's plan for your life— to help make disciples of all nations (Mt 28:18-19).** *You are to communicate Christianity to commission others to teach more still. When you act in this way, you work to extend the body of Christ around the world.*

Like Andy, have you led someone astray by accident? Give an example.

_____

_____

_____

_____

**Matthew 28:18-19**
Then Jesus came to them and said, "All authority in heaven and on earth has been given to me. 19) Therefore go and make disciples of all nations, baptizing them in the name of the Father and of the Son and of the Holy Spirit"

*Opie didn't want to learn—which made Helen not want to teach. But the Lord wants his people to do both. As a teacher, introduce the Good News to new believers. As a student, become a disciple to accomplish good works.* **Neither must discourage the other so that the church can be built up (Eph 4:11-12).**

Like Opie, have you discouraged teaching by resisting learning? Give an example.

_____

_____

_____

_____

> Ephesians 4:11-12
> It was he who gave some to be apostles, some to be prophets, some to be evangelists, and some to be pastors and teachers, 12) to prepare God's people for works of service, so that the body of Christ may be built up

Like Helen, have you tried to teach someone who didn't want to be taught? Give an example.

_____

_____

_____

_____

*Barney wanted everyone to think he knew everything—but he didn't want to tell them anything just yet. Similarly, Christians sometimes feel we should have all the answers before we communicate our message.* **Remember, the most important lesson is also the simplest: salvation comes from God the Father through Jesus Christ the Son (Jn 3:16).**

> John 3:16
> "For God so loved the world that he gave his one and only Son, that whoever believes in him shall not perish but have eternal life."

Like Barney, have you wanted to teach but felt you lacked knowledge? Give an example.

_____

_____

_____

_____

# Action

## *Get Out Your Bullet...*

2 TIMOTHY 2:24

***And the Lord's servant must not quarrel; instead, be must be kind
to everyone, able to teach, not resentful.*** *(NIV)*

> **1 Timothy 5:17**
> The elders who direct
> the affairs of the church well
> are worthy of double honor,
> especially those
> whose work is preaching
> and teaching.

> **James 3:1**
> Not many of you should
> presume to be teachers,
> my brothers, because
> you know that we
> who teach will be
> judged more strictly.

Good teaching can save lives. Bad teaching turns
others from truth. God's servants make good
teachers because they lead with kindness.
***Indeed, teaching and preaching are
similar in nature (1 Ti 5:17).*** *While
teachers offer explanation of the truth,
preachers encourage application to daily life.
In either case, teaching should never be taken lightly.*
***Because your example affects others, teachers are
judged more strictly (Jas 3:1).*** *As you teach, check your
effect on those that listen.*

How will God teach you?

_____

_____

_____

_____

_____

How will you teach others?

_____

_____

_____

_____

_____

Why will you be careful what you teach?

_____

_____

_____

_____

_____

_____

Have you taught someone wrong?  How can you correct that?

_____

_____

_____

_____

_____

_____

# From your friends at

# Primetime Parable Ministries

*Want to know what's next?*

*Want to hear when it's out?*

*Other questions or comments?*

Then call us at
**1-877-GOD-IN TV**
*(1-877-463-4688).*

*We look forward to serving you!*

Blessings,

Stephen Skelton
Primetime Parable Ministries

---

# DEDICATION:
## *Father*
## *Son*
## *Holy Spirit*